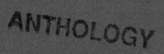

VERSE AHOY

EARLY AUSTRALIAN NURSERY RHYMES

VERSE AHOY

EARLY AUSTRALIAN NURSERY RHYMES

Selected by Robert Holden
illustrated by Heather Potter

Angus&Robertson
An imprint of HarperCollins*Publishers*

To Mark, family and friends — H.P.
For Sean and Emma Prater— R.H.

AN ANGUS & ROBERTSON BOOK
An imprint of HarperCollinsPublishers

First published in Australia in 1993 by
CollinsAngus&Robertson Publishers Pty Limited
A division of HarperCollinsPublishers (Australia) Pty Limited
25 Ryde Road, Pymble NSW 2073, Australia
HarperCollinsPublishers (New Zealand) Limited
31 View Road, Glenfield, Auckland 10, New Zealand
HarperCollinsPublishers Limited
77-85 Fulham Palace Road, London W6 8JB, United Kingdom

Initial design concept by P. Mark Jackson.

National Library of Australia
Cataloguing-in-Publication data:
Verse ahoy.
ISBN 0 207 18014 8.
1. Nursery rhymes, English. 2. Folk poetry, Australian. I. Holden, Robert. II. Potter, Heather.
398.8
Printed in Hong Kong
5 4 3 2 1
97 96 95 94 93

Introduction

Perhaps you will be surprised to learn that to that vast menagerie of traditional nursery rhymes — which includes blind mice, an amorous frog, lost sheep and a cat with a fiddle — can be added Australian creatures such as leaping, laughing kangaroos, fearsome bunyips and clever rabbits who outsmart the dingo!

In 1788 approximately 40 children under twelve years of age arrived in the First Fleet, and no doubt in this alien environment they, like their elders, sometimes turned for consolation to the rhymes, songs, lullabies and hymns of their homeland. It is, however, difficult to know just how well traditional English nursery rhymes survived the long sea journey last century and how secure the oral tradition remained.

Molesworth Jeffery, a minor mid-nineteenth-century literary figure in Tasmania, has left us with a touching look at English-born parents attempting to pass on the nursery tradition of their childhood to young colonists:

> *The Author, while sitting one Winter's evening beside his Family-hearth, was striving to recall old Nursery Rhymes. Amongst sundry antique songs that he endeavoured to vivify anew in his memory for the benefit of his Bairns, was the one commencing with 'Twinkle, twinkle, little Star'. But familiar as the first lines of that Composition may sound to all whose early life has been passed in England, neither the Author nor his Wife was able to recite more than two commencing stanzas ...* (1862)

Fifty years later the *Bulletin* sought to encourage national interest in the composition of distinctly Australian nursery rhymes by organising a competition in 1917. This call to take up literary and imaginative arms met with widespread interest, and 1000 entries were received in six weeks. Various examples were printed in the *Bulletin,* and for Christmas that year a booklet of 14 examples with illustrations by Norman Lindsay and others was published.

Some of these rhymes, together with others from equally forgotten sources, are gathered here to tempt and delight a new audience of young Australians.

Robert Holden
Sydney 1993

I HAD A LITTLE PONY

I had a little pony,
His name was Dapple Gray.
I sent him down to Melbourne
To win the Cup one day.

He couldn't beat the favourite,
For the favourite's hard to beat.
And now he pulls a milk cart
Along a Sydney street.

E. R.

THE LOCUST

I had a little locust
No bigger than my thumb.
I put him in a matchbox,
And there I bade him drum.

I opened up the matchbox,
To see if he was there —
'Buzz!' went the locust,
And flew into the air.

L. H. Allen

Ding Dong Bell

Ding dong bell,
Pussy's in the well,
'Twas all the water
We had got,
And now we'll have
To waste the lot.

E. R.

Greedy Guy

Greedy, greedy, greedy Guy,
Gobbled Granny's gooseberry pie.
Sour and tart was Granny's pie
Sorry and sad was Greedy Guy.

Harold Charles

I WANT TO BE LIKE CAPTAIN COOK

I want to be like Captain Cook
And sail the stormy sea —
From Manly round to Watson's Bay
And back to Circular Quay.

I will not be a farmer, but
A sailor bold and brave —
Instead of riding fences,
I shall plough the raging wave.

D. H. Souter

Goosey Goosey Gander

Goosey Goosey Gander,
Whither do you wander?
Your place is in the poultry yard
And not on the verandah.

E. R.

There Now

Helen

Macpherson

O'Sullivan

Brown

liked to see herself

upside down!

It was not proper to stand

on her head,

so she stood on the billabong

bank instead.

For, there in the water,

upside down

was —

Brown.

O'Sullivan

Macpherson

Helen

D. H. Souter

Clippity Clippity Clop

Clippity, clippity, clippity-clop,
Round by the stock-route
The creek and the crop.

Galloping horses and galloping dogs,
Dodging the rabbit-holes,
Jumping the logs.

When they get tired the
Horses will stop,
Then, we'll come home again,
Clippity-clop.

D. H. Souter

Little Miss Muffet

Little Miss Muffet
Arose from her tuffet
To box with the old kangaroo.

There came a big wombat
To join in the combat,
And little Miss Muffet withdrew.

E. R.

Little Billjim Aussie Boy

Little Billjim, Aussie boy,
Ate bananas with great joy.

Mother, frowning, said to him:
'Leave some room for dinner, Jim.'

Reaching for another bunch,
Billjim said, 'This *is* my lunch.'

D. H. Souter

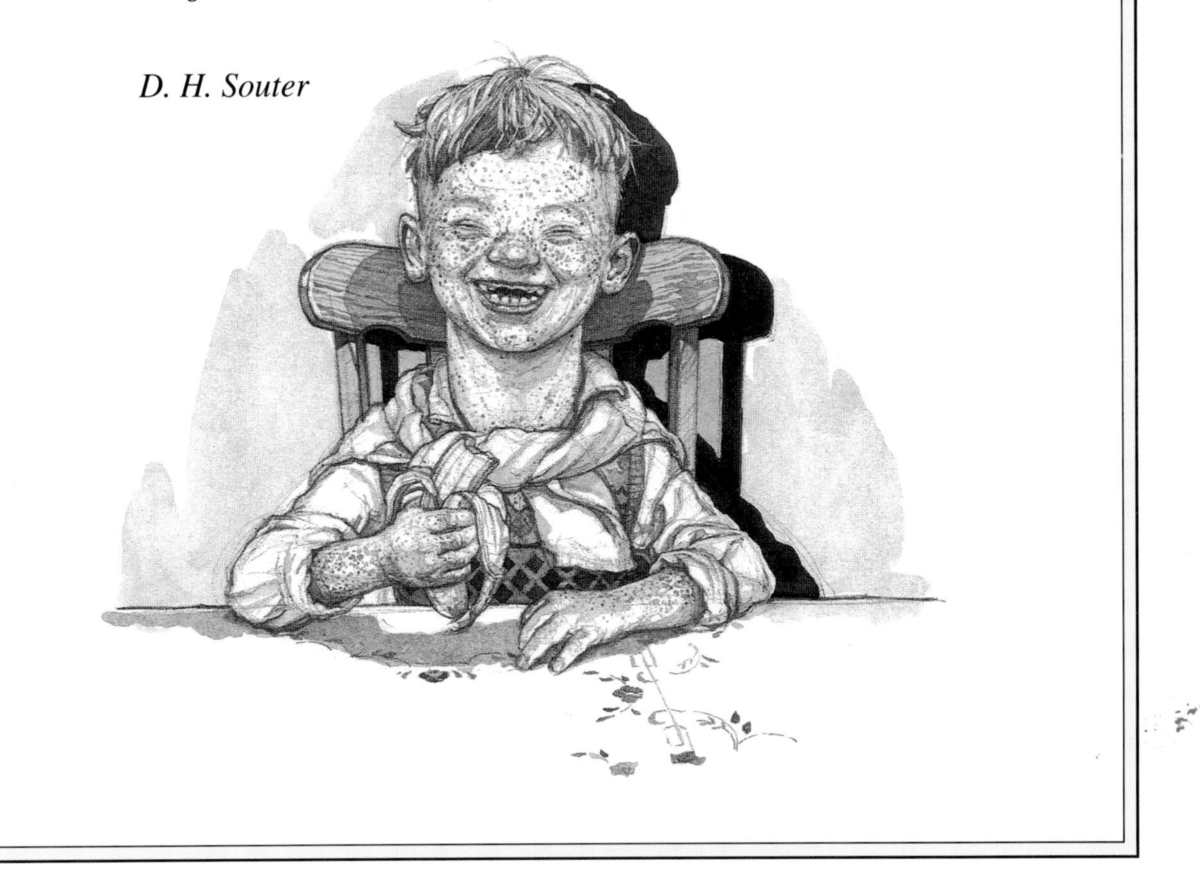

DIGGER, OUR CAT

Digger, our cat,
Is not very good.
He will not behave
As a good cat should.

He sleeps all the day
And has other bad habits.
He eats little chickens
And blue tongues and rabbits.

He fights with the dogs
And stays out all night.
Dad says 'He'll get shot
And —
serve
him
right!'

D. H. Souter

CLEVER SANDY

Sandy is a shearer
Who has shorn so many sheep
He does not need to keep awake —
He shears them in his sleep.

That isn't Sandy snoring,
It's only Sandy shoring.
He is so smart at shearing sheep
That he can shear them in his sleep.

D. H. Souter

The Man from Menindie

The man from Menindie
Was counting sheep;
He counted so many
He went to sleep.

He counted by threes
And he counted by twos;
The rams and the lambs
And the wethers and ewes.

He counted a thousand,
A hundred and ten …
And when he woke up
He'd to count them again!

D. H. Souter

Joseph and James

Joseph and James were such nice little boys,
Jigsaws and chess were their favourite toys.
They never played vulgar or dangerous games;
Such nice little boys were Joseph and James.

Peter and Paul were rougher than bags,
Their hair always tousled, their clothing in rags.
If anyone anywhere heard of a brawl,
They knew where to look for Peter and Paul.

D. H. Souter

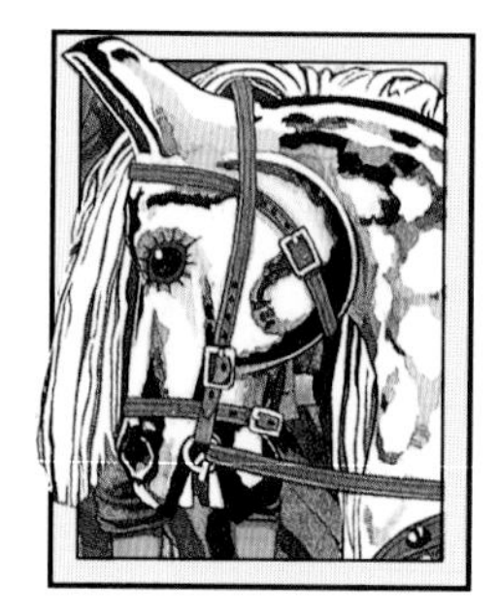

Muster Muster

Muster muster all of a cluster
Bring in the sheep to be shorn.
Bluster fluster southerly buster
Poppity's pants are torn.

'Tupp Mann'

There was a Little Rabbit

There was a little rabbit
That was hiding in his burrow,
When the dingo came and told him
To expect him there tomorrow.

But the rabbit thought he'd rather
That the dingo didn't meet him,
So he found another burrow
And the dingo didn't eat him!

D. H. Souter

Hush-a-bye Baby

Hush-a-bye baby, on the tree top,
Grasshoppers ate up the whole of our crop.

When the drought breaks the rabbits will come.
Hush-a-bye baby, the outlook is glum.

E. R.

SAMMY THE SWAGGIE

Sammy the swaggie has a big brown swag,
A little black billy and a white tucker bag,
A blue cattle-dog and a very red nose,
And they all go with him wherever he goes.

D. H. Souter

Bibliography

'I Had a Little Pony' by E. R. from *Bulletin,* November 1908.

'The Locust' by Leslie H. Allen from *Billy-Bubbles* (Melbourne, 1924).

'Ding Dong Bell' by E. R. from *Bulletin,* November 1908.

'Greedy Guy' by Harold Charles from *Australian Nursery Rhymes* (Melbourne, 1945)

'I Want to Be Like Captain Cook' by D. H. Souter from *Young Australia,* June 1928.

'Goosey Goosey Gander' by E. R. from *Bulletin,* November 1908.

'There Now' by D. H. Souter from *Bush Babs* (Sydney, 1933).

'Clippety Clippety Clop' by D. H. Souter from *Young Australia,* May 1928.

'Little Miss Muffet' by E. R. from *Bulletin,* November 1908.

'Little Billjim Aussie Boy' by D. H. Souter from *Bush Babs* (Sydney, 1933).

'Digger, Our Cat' by D. H. Souter from *Young Australia,* September 1928.

'Clever Sandy' by D. H. Souter from *Bush Babs* (Sydney, 1933).

'The Man from Menindie' by D. H. Souter from *Australian Nursery Rimes* (Sydney, 1917).

'Joseph and James' by D. H. Souter from *Bush Babs* (Sydney, 1933).

'Muster Muster' by 'Tupp Mann' from *Australian Nursery Rimes* (Sydney, 1917).

'There Was a Little Rabbit' by D. H. Souter from *Australian Nursery Rimes* (Sydney, 1917).

'Hush-a-bye Baby' by E. R. from *Bulletin,* November 1908.

'Sammy the Swaggie' by D. H. Souter from *Bush Babs* (Sydney, 1933).